Gregory McDonald

The Berenstain Bears®
GET JEALOUS

Stan & Jan Berenstain

A GOLDEN BOOK · NEW YORK
Western Publishing Company, Inc., Racine, Wisconsin 53404

ISBN: 0-307-23177-1

It was Brother Bear's birthday and
he was having a party. Brother blew
out the candles on his birthday cake
with one blow.

Now it was time for him to get
presents. Brother got many
presents.

He got some books.

He got a soccer ball.

He got a model airplane kit.

But best of all
was the present he got
from Mama Bear and
Papa Bear. It was a
two-wheel bike—a big,
beautiful two-wheel bike.

When everybody sang
"Happy Birthday" to
Brother Bear, Sister did
not sing. She did not sing
because she was jealous.

She wasn't jealous of
the books,

or the soccer ball,

or the model airplane
kit.

She was jealous of the
big, beautiful two-wheel
bike.

After the party, Brother
Bear rode his new bike
around the Bear's tree
house. Sister Bear tried
to catch up with him on
her trike. But Brother
rode past her like she
was standing still.

"Wow!" he shouted.
"Watch this! Look how fast
I can go!"

Sister Bear got so jealous, she couldn't stand it. Mama followed her into the house.

"Sister," said Mama, "I
think you have been bitten by
the green-eyed monster."

"The green-eyed monster?"
Sister said. "What's that?"

"The green-eyed monster is the part of us that gets jealous," said Mama. "It is the green-eyed monster that is making you jealous of Brother's two-wheel bike." Sister Bear looked out of the window. Brother was still riding around and around the tree house.

"It isn't fair!" said Sister. "Why can't *I* have a two-wheel bike?"

"Because," said Mama, "you are not ready for a two-wheel bike. A two-wheel bike is a bit too tall and your legs are a bit too short."

"Well, it just isn't fair," said Sister.

Sister had many nice things. She had dolls and a dollhouse.

She had skates and a jump rope.

She had her trike, of course.

But when you are jealous, the things you have look small next to the things you don't have.

Later that night, just as Sister was about to fall asleep, she had a visitor— a very strange visitor. It was a cub that looked just like Sister Bear, except that the visitor had green eyes and little horns on her head.

"I know who you are," said Sister. "You are the green-eyed monster."

"Never mind about that," said the visitor. "Come. I will show you how to get a two-wheel bike of your own. All you have to do is show Mama Bear and Papa Bear that you are ready."

Then the visitor helped Sister onto the bike and gave her a big push.

Off went Sister on Brother's big,
beautiful two-wheel bike. Around
and around the tree house she rode.
Faster and faster.

But the bike *was* a bit too tall and
her legs *were* a bit too short.

The bike began to wiggle.
The bike began to wobble.
Crash went the bike into
a big rock! Sister flew
through the air. Brother's
big, beautiful two-wheel bike
flew into a hundred pieces.

"Mama! Papa!" screamed
Sister.

But the sound that woke Mama and
Papa was not the sound of a crash. It
was the sound of Sister Bear waking
up from a bad dream.

"I'm sorry! I'm sorry! My legs *were* too short and the bike *was* too tall. I broke Brother's big, beautiful bike into a hundred pieces!"

"But it was just a dream, my dear," said Mama.

"Brother's bike is fine," said
Papa.

Sister looked out the window.
There was Brother's bike all in
one piece.

Brother was sorry that Sister had a bad dream. The next day he put training wheels on his new bike so she could try it out. She did pretty well, but the two-wheel bike *was* a bit too tall and her legs *were* a bit too short.

"You were right, Mama,"
she said. "I am not ready
for a two-wheel bike.

"But I will tell you what I *am* ready for. I *am* ready for that green-eyed monster. If she visits me again, I will send her on her way!"